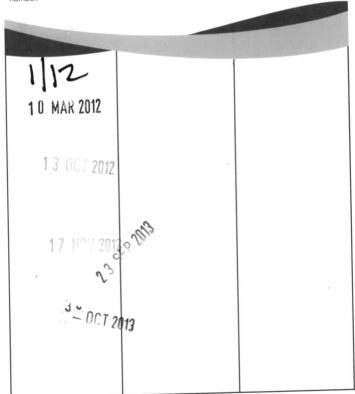

First published in Great Britain in 2011
by Boxer Books Limited
www.boxerbooks.com

Text copyright © 2011 Katy Kit
Illustrations copyright © 2011 Tom Knight

The rights of Katy Kit to be identified as the author and
Tom Knight as the illustrator of this work have been asserted by them
in accordance with the Copyright, Designs and Patents Act, 1988.

ISBN 978-1-907152-25-2

1 3 5 7 9 10 8 6 4 2

Printed in Great Britain

All of our papers are sourced from managed forests and renewable resources.

Mermaid Mysteries

Jasmine

and the
Treasure Chest

Written by **Katy Kit**

Illustrated by Tom Knight

Boxer Books

To Isabella,
who swims like a mermaid.

Contents

CHAPTER 1

Friends Forever

It was a chilly autumn morning in
Mermaid Bay. Jasmine, Melody and
Sula were at Gull Rock waiting for
their friend, Rosa, to arrive.

"Listen. This will make you laugh,"
said Jasmine. "Why *did* the lobster
blush?"

"I don't know," said Melody. "Why did the lobster blush?"

"Because the sea-weed!"

"That's revolting," cried Sula, laughing.

"It's silly," said Melody. "Everyone knows lobsters can't blush."

"OK. I'll tell you another," said Jasmine, determined to make Melody laugh. "What's another name for a mermaid?"

Melody and Sula shook their heads.

"A deep-SHE fish!"

This time they both laughed.

"There! Made you smile," said Jasmine brightly. She loved to make her friends laugh.

"Where *has* Rosa got to?" said Melody. "It's not like her to be late."

"There she is," said Sula, pointing at something green, flashing through the water. Swiftly Rosa reached the rock.

"You're late," said Melody.

"I'm sorry. Follow me and I'll show you why," Rosa replied.

"But we're supposed to be helping the water fairies in the Underwater Gardens today," said Melody.

"Yes, but that can wait," replied Rosa. "Come on. Hurry!"

So the three mermaids dived into the sea and joined Rosa as she led them across the bay to Rainbow Falls.

Once there, Jasmine, Melody and Sula waited to see what would happen.

"We meet again," said a voice. The mermaids looked around.

"Coral!" all three shrieked, as a beautiful mermaid swam towards them. Coral was Rosa's cousin from the South Sea. She had visited Mermaid Bay earlier that summer, but there had been no plans for her to

return quite so soon.

"What in the sea monsters are you doing here?" asked Jasmine.

"Well," said Coral, "there's good and bad news. Which do you want first?"

"Not too bad, I hope," replied Melody, looking concerned.

"I'm afraid it is," Coral said. "Over the past few weeks, the South Sea has seen some terrible storms. Many sea folk lost their homes and had to find new ones. Then last week, a giant wave started to gather far out at sea. By the time it crashed

into our bay, it had grown enormous.
It was so large that it ripped all the sea
plants from the ground and smashed
the rocks and reef into a thousand
pieces. Now there is no food or shelter.
Everyone has had to leave."

"How sad, Coral," said Sula. "You
must have been very frightened. What
are you going to do now?"

"Well, that's where the good news comes in," said Coral, brightening up. "I've come to stay in Mermaid Bay, at least until things have settled down."

"That's fantastic news!" said Sula.

"It's always such fun when you're around," said Jasmine.

"We'll find you a new home in no time," said Rosa.

"Well, first let me give you these," said Coral beaming.

From out of her purse, she took four

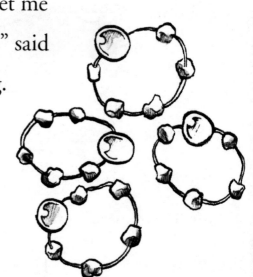

beautiful bracelets. Each one was made from a delicate strand of silver sea silk, and was threaded with five glittering sea nuggets and a stunning pearl. "I hope you like them," she said shyly.

Now, all mermaids love jewels. They can't help it – they're just made that way. But these pearls were no ordinary pearls. Earlier that summer, when Coral visited Mermaid Bay, the friends won a necklace at the Midsummer Carnival, which they had given to Coral for helping them to win.

"The pearls are from the necklace,"

said Jasmine. "How thoughtful of you, Coral, to give us one each."

"They're friendship bracelets," said Coral.

"Friends forever!" exclaimed Rosa. "Yes, that's right."

The mermaids put on the bracelets, and then holding their palms together, shouted, "Friends forever!"

"Oh, p-lease," said Myrtle, swimming up to them.

"I think I'm going to be sick," Muriel joined in.

Myrtle and Muriel were twin mermaids from Mermaid Bay Merschool. They seemed to enjoy making fun of the younger girls.

"You're not still showing off about

 the carnival, are you? You only won because you were the youngest team," continued Myrtle.

"Well, at least we had fun," said Rosa, defensively.

Myrtle and Muriel blushed, remembering the silly argument they

had had during the competition.

"Come on, everyone, we should make our way over to the Underwater Gardens," said Melody. "It's open day tomorrow and the fairies need our help."

Glad to have an excuse to leave Myrtle and Muriel behind, all five mermaids swam swiftly off.

CHAPTER 2

The Underwater Gardens

The Underwater Gardens were full
of coral and plants, many of which
had long since disappeared from the
surrounding sea. They were looked
after by the water fairies, who, every
season, opened them up to the sea

folk of Mermaid Bay. The tiny water fairies loved the gardens, and treated everything that grew there with respect. Sometimes the plants became overgrown, and this was why the young mermaids had offered their help. A large stone arch holding a pair of rusty gates led into the grounds. Rosa rang the bell.

"My, you've grown," sang a familiar voice.

The mermaids looked around, but they couldn't see anyone.

"I'm up here," came the voice again, "by King Neptune's head."

"Queenie!"
said Rosa with
glee, looking
up at the stone
carving on top of the arch. Queenie
fluttered her tiny wings and flew
down.

"Let me have a good look at you
all. What a tail, Rosa. It's turned a
beautiful shade of green. And Sula!
Why, your hair reaches right down
to your waist, now. Melody, you're
wearing glasses. All that reading I
shouldn't wonder. I haven't forgotten
you, either, Jasmine. Still up to your

25

tricks? I often think of the time you rolled in the sand and posed as a statue. It took us an age to find you, and there you were, in front of our very eyes, all along!"

Everyone laughed.

"So who are you, dear?" asked Queenie, turning to Coral.

Coral explained that she was Rosa's cousin and told her why she had come to Mermaid Bay.

"Well, you're most welcome. We do have the odd storm, especially around this time of year, but, usually, they're not too bad. So, are you ready for some work?"

"We certainly are," said Rosa. "Just tell us what to do."

Queenie raised her wand and waved it in front of the entrance. The water fizzed and, slowly, the rusty gates opened. Inside, the gardens were dark, and full of overgrown plants.

Soon the mermaids were busy. Rosa and Coral started by tying back

long trails of sea
bracken. Then
they cut down
the overgrown
plants.
Melody
and Sula
pulled up
fresh shoots
of seaweed
before
moving on
to clean the
many garden
statues.

Jasmine swept up
shells from the
sea floor.
For a few
hours, the
mermaids
lost
themselves
in this
world.
That
is, until
Jasmine got
bored.

29

"Come and play hide-and-seek with me, Sula," she demanded. But Sula was happy cleaning the statues.

"What about you, Melody?" she asked.

But Melody was talking to Queenie about the history of the Underwater Gardens. "The gardens have been here for as long as King Neptune – and he's as old as the sea itself," said Queenie.

"What were they like in the olden days?" asked Melody.

"Well, I don't really know," replied Queenie, "but I do remember that when I was a young fairy, the gardens were adorned with sparkling jewels. It was quite a magical place then."

"That must have been wonderful," said Rosa, her eyes shining. "What happened to them all?"

"No one is sure. Over time, they just disappeared. It's such a shame."

The mermaids agreed.

"Queenie," said Sula, who was gazing at a pair of particularly striking statues.

"Can you tell me who these two are?"

Queenie, followed by the mermaids, fluttered up to take a look.

"Ahhh. Now this is Aroona," she said, looking at the statue of a mermaid. "And the human is Sir Topaz. See he has legs, rather than a tail? That's what makes him different from us – why he has to live on land."

"Poor man," said Sula.

"Yes, and poor Aroona too, so the story goes," said Queenie. "But we'll leave that for another time. Come on, back to work everyone. There's still a lot to be done."

So the mermaids carried on. As they cleared away the larger plants, light filtered in, and the autumn gardens sprung to life. Little flowers opened, sea fans stretched out and, for the first time in months, the seaweed let their tendrils dance free. At the end of the day, everyone was exhausted.

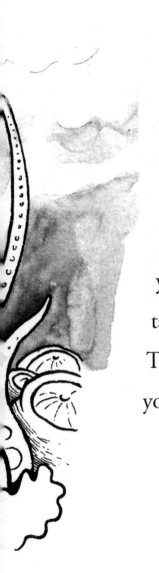

"Well done, girls. It looks wonderful. Thank you for helping," said Queenie. "Now, why don't we all swim out to Gull Rock and watch the sunset. If you like I'll tell you the tale of Aroona and Sir Topaz as a reward for all your hard work."

CHAPTER 3

Aroona and Sir Topaz

"Right. Everyone comfortable?" asked Queenie. She was perched in the middle of Gull Rock. The mermaids, who surrounded her, nodded, and waited patiently for her to begin.

"Once upon a time, many years ago,

there was a beautiful mermaid called
Aroona. She lived here, in Mermaid
Bay. Aroona had long red hair the
colour of autumn kelp, deep blue eyes
the colour of summer sea and a silver-
grey tail as cold as winter water. Every
day at sunrise, Aroona would leave the
watery depths and swim ashore. There
she would meet with a kind and
gentle man called
Sir Topaz."

Sula sighed.
Rosa lay her
head down on
some sea moss. Queenie went on.

"Sir Topaz was very much in love
with Aroona, and every time he saw
her, he gave her a jewel. Now, as we all
know, mermaids love their jewels, and
Aroona was no
exception.
So Aroona
stored
them in
a treasure
chest, which
she kept hidden
somewhere in Mermaid Bay. No
mermaid had ever been happier. One
day, however, Sir Topaz told Aroona

he could no longer live without her. He asked Aroona to leave her underwater life and come to live with him on land."

The mermaids gasped.

"Now, I'm not sure whether you know this or not, but if for any reason a mermaid wishes to leave the sea, she loses her beautiful tail and grows legs. And once the tail has gone, it never grows back."

"Surely she didn't allow that to happen?" said Jasmine, shocked at the thought. The others agreed.

"Well, Aroona had grown to love Sir

Topaz She loved him so much, in fact, that she *did* agree to leave. But still having her mermaid's desire for jewels, she explained to him that before she left she must go back one last time to collect her chest."

The mermaids smiled. This was something they did understand.

"So, the couple arranged to meet that very evening at sunset, over at Smugglers' Cove."

"I still can't believe she'd really want to go – leave the sea and her home forever. How terrible," said Coral.

"Falling in love can make people do some very strange things," said Queenie. "Anyway, that evening, as

Aroona made her way towards the cove, although the water was calm on the surface, the water beneath was in turmoil."

"That's called a rip tide, isn't it?" said Melody.

"I believe so," said Queenie, "you *are* a clever one, aren't you?"

She paused then went on. "So, Sir Topaz waited and waited, unaware that Aroona, who was already losing her scales, was struggling to reach him. The current was so strong that Aroona didn't make it to Smugglers' Cove. She was never seen again. And Sir Topaz? He went home with a broken heart and never returned to the sea."

For a moment the mermaids were silent.

"Poor Aroona," said Sula, "she must have been so frightened. I wonder what happened to her."

"It's just an old sea tale," said Queenie, "no one really knows whether it's true or not. Although, there are *some* who say that, even today, somewhere in Mermaid Bay is a trail of scales that leads to her treasure chest."

"Really?" said Rosa. "How exciting! I'd love to find it. Why don't we get up early tomorrow and try."

"Oh, yes. Let's!" said Coral. Sula and Melody nodded enthusiastically.

Jasmine stared at her friends in disbelief. "It's only a story. Didn't you hear what Queenie said? I can't believe you're all taking it so seriously."

"You never know, Jasmine. There

could be something in it," said Sula.

Jasmine laughed. "Well count me out, I've better things to do."

"Suit yourself," said Rosa. "But don't come begging when we find the jewels."

She turned to the others. "Let's meet at Crystal Grotto tomorrow at seven, before anyone else is about."

CHAPTER 4

The Scale Trail

The following morning, Rosa, Coral, Melody and Sula arrived at Crystal Grotto, keen to start their search.

"I've been thinking," said Melody, "to save time, we should split up. I've been to see the Sandman, and he's loaned me these four small sea horns."

She gave
them out and
continued,
"If anyone
finds even the

hint of a trail, blow your horn and
the rest of us will come."

"You're taking this very seriously,
Melody," said Rosa, amused.

"Well, you want to find the treasure
chest too, don't you?"

"Any other tips?" asked Sula.

"Just look for anything unusual,
anything out of the ordinary," Melody

replied. "Right, are we ready? I'll start over at Rainbow Falls."

"I'll go to the Merschool," said Sula.

"I'll look around Gull Rock," said Coral.

"And I'll stay here," said Rosa.

So Melody, Sula and Coral swam off. But after only a few minutes, they heard the clear high note of a horn sound out. It was coming from Crystal

Grotto. Feeling very excited, they returned as fast as they could.

"You'll never believe it, but I think I've found the trail," laughed Rosa. "I noticed that a large group of crabs were gathered behind this rock. Thinking it unusual, I swam over, only to find them holding these scales in their claws. Look there are masses of them. They're leading towards Splash Lagoon.

The mermaids followed Rosa's

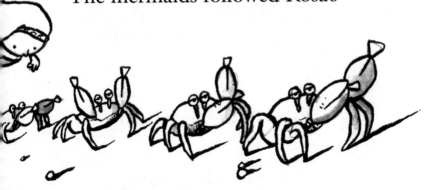

pointing finger. Sure enough, a trail of scales, flashing and glinting in the light, led far into the distance.

"Well done, Rosa!" said Melody. "Good detecting. Let's go."

As quick as a flash, the four mermaids were following the silver trail across Sandy Bottom. In no time at all, they arrived at Splash Lagoon. But the trail didn't end there . . .

"Oh no," said Sula, "it's leading to Five Fathom Forest now. I don't think we should go in there. There are sea monsters and all kinds of strange creatures."

But the others were too excited to stop now.

"We'll look after you, Sula. Come on, hold my hand," said Melody.

The four mermaids were off again, racing towards the forest. As they entered, everything went dark, and tall strands of sea grass clung to their bodies. Sula started to tremble.

"Don't worry, Sula," said Melody, "look, they're leading us out again –

this time towards the Underwater Gardens. Surely the treasure chest can't be there?"

"Let's go and see," said Coral. "This is just so exciting! I can't wait to tell Jasmine."

In no time at all, they arrived at the Underwater Gardens. Today, the gates were open and crowds of sea folk were milling around.

"Oh dear," said Rosa, "if the treasure chest is in here, anyone could find it!"

"The trail doesn't end here, though," said Melody. "Look, it's headed

towards Rainbow Falls. Hurry!"

Again the mermaids sped across the seabed. Soon they felt the cascade of water from above.

"Look, the trail leads behind the falls. Let's see

what's there," said Melody.

As the four mermaids swam into the waterfall, the bubbling water made it difficult for them to see. Gradually, from behind a rock, a mermaid appeared. She had long red hair and was carrying a treasure chest.

"It's Aroona," whispered Melody to the others, "swim slowly; we don't want to frighten her away."

The mermaids' hearts were pounding. It seemed so unreal. But as they got closer, they noticed that 'Aroona' was starting to smile. Soon she burst out laughing.

"Jasmine!" screamed Melody,

"You should see your faces," replied Jasmine, plucking long strands of red seaweed from her head.

"I can't believe you've done this," continued Melody, outraged.

"I can't believe you fell for it!" laughed Jasmine.

"I was frightened back there,

Jasmine," said Sula. "You led us into Five Fathom Forest. That could have been dangerous."

"Only a little. And you have to admit," she said, still laughing, "it was all good fun."

"Well it isn't now," said Rosa, "is it?" And she turned to the others. They shook their heads. "We're disappointed Jasmine. Come on, let's go to the Underwater Gardens and cheer ourselves up."

CHAPTER 5

Stormy Waters

Still chuckling to herself, Jasmine watched the others swim away. It's a shame they didn't think it was funny, she thought. Oh well, they'll have forgotten about it tomorrow. She looked at the treasure chest, which she'd dropped by the rock.

"I suppose I'd better return it to the Sandman," she said out loud.

But as Jasmine swam towards the chest, she noticed something sticking out of the sand. She picked it up. It was a silver-grey scale. But this scale wasn't shiny and new like the ones she had used for her trail; it was dull and old. In fact, it looked as if it had been at the bottom of the sea for years. Surely these can't be Aroona's scales, thought Jasmine. After all, it was just a story, wasn't it?

She brushed the sand from another scale, then another, then another. It was starting to look like a trail. Wow! The others will be so excited, thought Jasmine. I can't wait to tell them.

Quickly she rushed to the Underwater Gardens where her friends were at the gates.

"Melody, Rosa, Sula, Coral – wait," Jasmine called.

The mermaids turned round.

"I know this sounds strange, but I think I've found Aroona's trail. Come with me and I'll show you."

"Not another practical joke, Jasmine?" said Melody.

"No. I promise it isn't," said Jasmine. "Come on. If we follow it, we might just find the treasure chest!"

"Sorry, Jasmine. We're not going to

be fooled again," said Sula. And the mermaids swam off into the gardens leaving Jasmine on her own.

"A treasure chest, you say," said another voice, "that sounds like fun. We'll come."

The voice belonged to Myrtle, who was swimming towards the gardens.

Muriel was following close behind.

"I'm not sure," said Jasmine, suspiciously. It was strange for Myrtle and Muriel to be offering their help. "I don't know where it will lead. We might never find the treasure chest."

"It's something to do," said Muriel, sounding bored.

Jasmine considered their offer. She

really didn't want to go alone. "OK then," she agreed. "Let's go."

So the three mermaids returned to Rainbow Falls. As they did, Jasmine told Myrtle and Muriel the story of Aroona and Sir Topaz and the lost treasure chest. Then they set off along the trail.

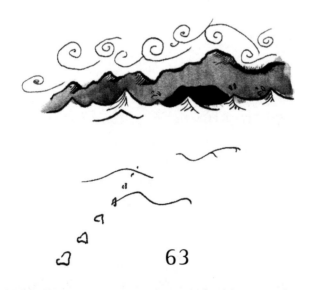

At first the mermaids moved slowly, making sure they didn't lose sight of the scales. But gradually they became easier to spot, and soon the mermaids were swimming swiftly along. After a while, the trail started to lead out of Mermaid Bay, towards the distant Smugglers' Cove. The sea was choppier here and the water felt cold.

"I've never been this far away from home before," said Jasmine, feeling anxious.

"I'm getting bored," said Myrtle, who was feeling worried too, but didn't want to admit it. "I want to go back."

"We're almost there, though," said
Jasmine. "Let's not give up."

"This is leading nowhere," said
Muriel. "You carry on if you like.
We're going back." And just like that,

Myrtle and Muriel turned round and swam away, leaving Jasmine alone.

But a storm was brewing and the water was surging and swirling about. Soon Jasmine was finding it difficult to swim. This is dangerous. I should go back, thought Jasmine. But if I do, the others will never believe me. I have to carry on.

Bravely Jasmine battled her way along the trail to Smugglers' Cove. But the force of the water was too strong, and in the end she gave up swimming against it. Rising to the surface, a huge wave crashed over her body. Before she knew what had happened, Jasmine was dragged down and thrown into an underwater cave. As the wave rushed back out, she clung on to a rock. At least here Jasmine could shelter from the angry sea.

CHAPTER 6

Queenie's Gift

Meanwhile, the rest of the mermaids were just leaving the Underwater Gardens when Myrtle and Muriel arrived. The storm had followed the twins in, and surging water was making it difficult for everyone to swim.

"Have you seen Jasmine?" Sula asked the older mermaids. "I'm worried about her being alone in this storm."

"We followed the trail with her, but got bored. Jasmine wanted to stay," answered Myrtle. "We left her a while ago swimming out to Smugglers' Cove."

"You left her alone, so far from Mermaid Bay?" said Rosa, aghast. "She's your friend. Why weren't you with her?" replied Muriel.

The mermaids looked embarrassed.

"So there *was* a trail?" asked Melody.

"Yes," said Myrtle, "of old grey
scales, just like she said."

"It wasn't a joke after all,"
said Coral flatly.

"Smugglers' Cove is very exposed.
The storm must be raging over there,"

said Melody with a worried frown.

"What do we do now?" Sula asked.
"We can't leave her on her own."

"I know," said Rosa. "Let's ask
Queenie if she can help."

So the mermaids fought their way

back into the gardens. There the water
fairies were sheltering beneath a huge
coral fan. Quickly they told Queenie
about Jasmine and the danger she was
in, all alone in the storm.

"Smugglers' Cove. That's a long way off. It will take you at least an hour to swim that far. There is another way of getting there, though," said Queenie, her eyes twinkling.

"How?" said Melody.

"Well, I have a magic shell. If you whisper into the shell and tell it where you want to go, it listens. Then, if you climb in, it takes you there. The trouble is, you have to be tiny, like me, to fit inside."

"Can you make us small, Queenie?" asked Melody. "Please."

"I can. If that's what you want."

The mermaids nodded. The storm was getting worse and they were all very worried about Jasmine.

"Follow me then, my dears," said Queenie, and she swam to the centre of the gardens. The mermaids followed. There on the seabed lay a pure white shell.

"Who's first?" asked Queenie.
Bravely Melody swam forwards.

Queenie took her magic wand,
dipped it into a pot of stardust and
waved it above Melody's head. As
the stardust fell, the water around
her began to swirl. When it stopped,
a miniature Melody
swam out.

"What do
I do now?"
she asked.

The others burst out laughing.

"What are you laughing at?"
asked Melody, looking uneasy.

"It's your voice," said Sula,
"it's very high."

"Come on," said Queenie, "let's

hurry. Swim inside the shell, Melody.
Rosa, your turn next."

When all the
mermaids were
inside the shell,
Queenie joined
them.

"I'd better come
too," she said. "You'll need to bring
Jasmine back in the shell, so you will
need my help,"

Inside, the shell was dark and quiet.
"Now we must tell it where we want
to go," said Queenie. All at once,
everyone started whispering.

"Smugglers' Cove.
Smugglers' Cove.
Smugglers' Cove."

The words echoed and ran into
each other, and soon all the mermaids
could hear was a jumble of letters.

Suddenly the shell
turned upside
down and
lurched
forwards.

The mermaids
tumbled out into the furious sea.

They looked around.

"Here we are," shouted Queenie,
"Smugglers' Cove. I'll wait with the
shell. You find Jasmine."

So the mermaids swam off through
the stormy sea. It was difficult, being
so small, but they stuck together and
looked about.

After a while, Rosa shrieked, "There she is. Over there, in that cave."

Jasmine was tired having spent so long battling against the surging water. Seeing the tiny mermaids swim up to her, she looked confused.

"I must be dreaming," she said. "You look just like my friends, only smaller."

"It is us, Jasmine," said Sula, "we've come to take you back to Mermaid Bay. Queenie's made us small so that we can travel in her magic shell. But never mind that. We need to get you out of here before this storm gets even worse."

"But we can't leave now," said Jasmine, looking upset. "This is where the trail ends, you see. This is where Aroona must have left her treasure chest."

"It's too dangerous," said Melody, "and Queenie's waiting for us. We shouldn't stay."

Just then, the water in the cave calmed. Out of the gloom swam a beautiful girl. She had long red hair, and legs, like a human. She was holding out a treasure chest.

Slowly she bent forwards and put the chest down.

"Am I dreaming?" asked Jasmine.

"No," said Melody, "I can see her too."

Then, without a word the girl turned and swam back into the gloom.

"It's the treasure chest!" exclaimed Jasmine. "That must have been Aroona."

"Or the ghost of Aroona," said Sula, shivering.

"Oh Jasmine," said Rosa, "we're so sorry for not believing you and letting you come all the way out here on your own."

"Don't worry," said Jasmine, "you're here now. It was my fault anyway for playing the joke on you in the first place. Come on, let's find out what's inside."

Carefully Jasmine lifted the lid. It was rusty and stuck a little before suddenly flying open to reveal its treasure. The mermaids gasped. Inside were the most wonderful jewels they had ever seen.

Rubies, diamonds, pearls, emeralds, opals and sapphires were heaped up on top of each other, sparkling and glistening as if they were new.

"I've never seen so many jewels," said Jasmine. "Whatever will we do with them all?"

"I've an idea," said Coral. "Why don't we give them to Queenie? She can use them to replace those that disappeared from the Underwater Gardens."

"That's a fantastic idea," said Jasmine, and the others all agreed.

"Come on. Let's go back to the shell and tell her. I'm tired. I want to go home."

The following day, once the magic
had worn off and they were back
to their normal size, the mermaids
returned to the Underwater
Gardens. They had been invited
by the water fairies to be the first
to admire the gardens now that,

once again, they were adorned with jewels.

"They look truly magical," said Jasmine, standing beneath the statue of Aroona.

"And it's all thanks to you, Jasmine," said the statue in a loud clear voice.

Jasmine leaped back in surprise. "The statue – it talked to me!" she exclaimed. Then she noticed that the other mermaids were laughing.

Just for a moment, Jasmine couldn't work out why.

Then suddenly she
let out a loud hoot of
laughter too.

"FOOLED YOU!"
her friends cried.

Here's a sneak preview
of another exciting
mermaid mystery

Rosa *and the* **Water Pony**

A midsummer carnival,
a beautiful pearl necklace
and a missing magical pony.

CHAPTER 1

The Crystal Grotto

With a flick of her tail, Rosa dived into the water. Melody, Sula and Jasmine stared at the bubbles on the surface, waiting for her to reappear. Soon enough, Rosa's head popped out. "Race you to Crystal Grotto,"

she called,
"last one
there's a sea
slug!" And,
with another
flick of her
tail, she was
gone.
Splish.
Splash.
Splosh.
Quickly, the
other three
mermaids leapt
in after her.

Soon, all four were speeding through the water, swishing their tails up and down as fast as they could. Rosa got there first – she always did – then Sula, then Jasmine, then Melody.

"Bad luck, Melody," said Jasmine. "Looks like you're the sea slug."

"Only because you knocked off my glasses with your crazy swimming," said Melody. "I couldn't see a thing!"

To find out what happens, buy your copy today.

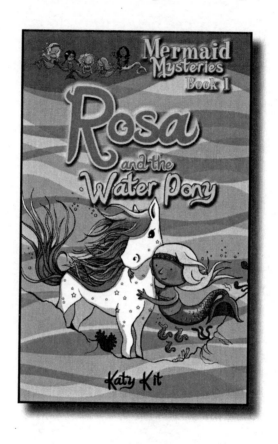